Lemonade Genie

Adrian Boote

Illustrated by Tim Archbold

ORCHARD BOOKS

Look out for the

Madcap Moonwood adventures!

The Lemonade Genie

The Ice Cream Cowboys

To the staff and pupils of
Sevenoaks Primary School A.B.

For Rosie and John T.A.

ORCHARD BOOKS
96 Leonard Street, London EC2A 4XD
Orchard Books Australia
14 Mars Road, Lane Cove, NSW 2066
First published in Great Britain in 2000
First paperback edition 2000

A CIP catalogue record for this book is available
from the British Library.
ISBN 1 84121 007 2 (hbk)
ISBN 1 84121 009 9 (pbk)
1 3 5 7 9 10 8 6 4 2 (hbk)
3 5 7 9 10 8 6 4 2 (pbk)
Printed in Great Britain

Contents

GLUE

1

The Exploding Lunch Box

Everyone at Moonwood County Primary School agreed: Colin Crumbly was the most disastrous person in the world.

"If there were gold medals for being disastrous, you, Colin Crumbly, would win every one," declared Mrs Stick, his teacher, one day. "And then, because you are Colin Crumbly, you would probably lose them, or break them, or swallow them, or get them stuck up your nose and sneeze them all over everybody."

The whole class laughed, and Colin Crumbly nodded his head sadly. Because Mrs Stick was right. That was *exactly* what Colin Crumbly would do.

Every day, Colin Crumbly lost things, broke things, dropped things, spilled things, tripped over things, fell into things, knocked things down, messed things up, got things confused . . . and generally left things looking as if they had been tormented by a herd of mad wildebeest.

And that was on a good day.

On this particular day, Colin Crumbly had been especially disastrous.

He had fallen out of bed, face-first into the bowl of soggy cornflakes he kept by the bed in case he got hungry during the night.

He had accidentally bitten off and swallowed the bristly bit of his toothbrush.

He had hiccuped at the breakfast table – so loudly and suddenly that his dad's false teeth shot out of his mouth, faster than a bullet from a gun, and shattered the kitchen window.

He had mistaken his dog Dumpster's tail for a piece of toast, and dunked the horrible hairy thing into his boiled egg.

He had set off for school wearing his pyjamas underneath his school uniform, his coat-hanger still in the back of his coat and fifteen feet of toilet roll trailing out of the back of his trousers.

He had blown his nose during school assembly – without a handkerchief. Everyone around him ducked out of the way to avoid getting splattered; fell over, and knocked everyone around *them* over, until the whole school had fallen over like dominoes.

All except Colin Crumbly.

"Sorry," he said. "Very sorry, everybody."

The day had started badly, but it was about to get much, much worse…

When the lunch-time bell rang, everyone in Mrs Stick's class except Colin Crumbly jumped up and shot out of the classroom as if they had scorpions in their underwear.

The reason was very simple. Nobody wanted to be around when Colin Crumbly opened his lunch box. Colin Crumbly was so disastrous it was terrifying to think what he could do with a lunch box. Colin Crumbly's lunch box was like an unexploded bomb. When the lid came off, anything could happen.

A can of something fizzy could spring out and spray the whole classroom with a cloud of thick, sweet stickiness.

A crisp packet could blow up and burst everywhere in a storm of stinky cheese and onionness. Sandwiches made of goodness-knows-what could leap out and splatter everywhere with all sorts of unspeakably horrible disgustingness.

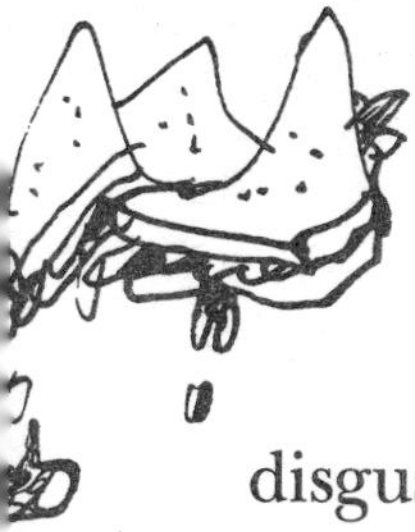

Colin Crumbly, the Grand Duke of Disaster, could make all these things happen. And even he didn't blame his classmates for wanting to run away from him as fast as possible.

But it still made him sad.

Just for once, Colin thought, as he peeled the lid off his lunch box, it would be nice to be *liked* by someone.

That day, Colin had a can of lemonade to drink with his banana and fish paste sandwiches. It was a fairly ordinary can of lemonade. There were no warning signs on it. There were no labels which read: *This lemonade can is absolutely not to be opened by Colin Crumbly.* And so, as Colin peeled back the ring-pull, he wasn't expecting anything extraordinary to happen.

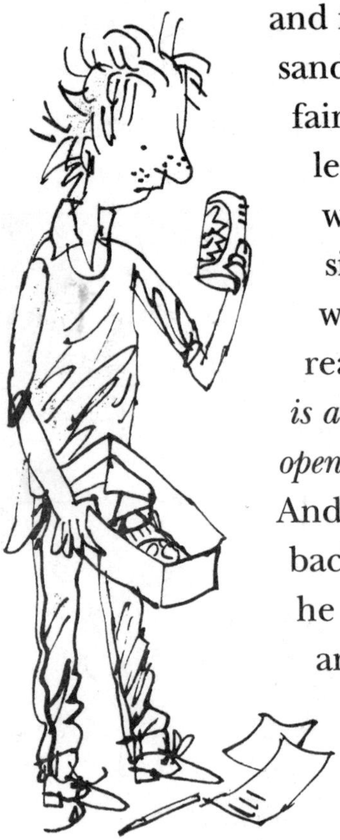

But something extraordinary did happen.

There was an explosion of billions of silver bubbles. There was a great hissing and rushing and gurgling noise, like the sound of a giant balloon that someone has let go of. And there was a flash of dazzling yellow light, so bright that it knocked Colin Crumbly clean off his chair and into the wastepaper-basket.

"Sorry, mate. Didn't mean to make you jump!" said a voice.

Colin wrenched and wrestled and wriggled until the wastepaper-basket let go of his bottom. Then he scrambled back into his chair.

He had spilt lemonade all down his trousers. His crisp packet had exploded and the air was full of thick, choky cheese and onion dust. A banana and fish paste sandwich had blasted from the lunch box and glued itself to Colin Crumbly's forehead.

But he didn't care about that now. Because something far more remarkable had happened.

"Wotcher, Colin. How are you diddling?"

Colin said nothing. He knew that if he tried to speak, his tongue would trip over itself and his teeth would tangle up. All he could do was let his jaw dangle helplessly and stare at the craziest-looking person he had ever seen.

2
The Nose-blowing Orchestra

There was a young man sitting on the corner of Colin's table. He was wearing a huge suit made of silver glitter which winked and sparkled under the classroom lights. He wore a dazzling lemon yellow shirt. Lemon yellow shoes. Lemon yellow-rimmed sunglasses. Big, dangly, lemon ear-rings. And he had lemon yellow hair, that stuck up in spikes as if someone had exploded it.

Colin couldn't be sure, but somehow he didn't think this young man was a teacher.

"Who are you?" asked Colin, carefully.

"I'm the Lemonade Genie," said the young man. "But you can call me Keith."

"Keith?" repeated Colin.

"That's right," said Keith. "Keith the Lemonade Genie. I just exploded out of your lemonade can."

"You're a genie . . . you came out of my lemonade can . . . and you're called Keith?" said Colin, not believing a word of it.

"That's it, Colin my old cock sparrow. Got it in one. Bright boy, you are. You'll be a brain surgeon one day."

"You're pulling my leg," said Colin. And he got up and backed slowly towards the classroom door. "Genies don't come out of lemonade cans. And genies aren't called Keith. And genies don't look like complete idiots with yellow hair and lemons in their ears."

"Oh, is that right, Colin?" said Keith, coolly. "Know a lot about genies, do you? Done the Genie Training Course, have you?"

"Aladdin's genie wasn't called Keith. And he came out of a lamp and wore a turban," said Colin, firmly.

"Ah, but Aladdin's just a fairy story," Keith smiled. "I'm real. And I may look like a complete idiot to you, Colin my little weasel, but truth is more idiotic than fiction."

"I don't believe you!" Colin exclaimed. And he decided to make a run for it. He crashed through the classroom door and hurtled along the corridor towards the playground.

Now, Colin Crumbly running was a peculiar sight. The foremost scientists in the land would have trouble working out how he did it. He always looked as if he were on the very point of toppling over.

His head wobbled violently, this way and that, as if it were about to drop off. His arms and legs flapped and flailed and seemed to be going in different directions. And behind him, he left a trail of disaster. Books and papers scattered. Chairs tipped up.

Doors flew open and crashed shut. Colin tore along the corridor like a small tornado, before tumbling down some steps nose-first into a puddle in the playground.

"So you won't be wanting your three wishes, then?" said Keith, who was already there, sitting on the bottom step waiting for him.

"Three wishes?" repeated Colin, getting up and peeling a lump of old chewing-gum off the end of his nose. "You mean, you're a proper almighty all-powerful genie who can give people whatever they ask for?"

"Sure. Well. Almost," said Keith. "I'm the most almighty all-powerful genie in the whole of Moonwood County Primary School, ain't I?"

Colin had to agree that Keith was probably right about that.

"See that seagull up there?" said Keith, nodding up to the sky. "I could turn that boring old seagull into a magnificent golden eagle – just by jiggling my eyebrow. Just you watch, Colin, my old cocker."

And Keith stared at the seagull and jiggled a lemon yellow eyebrow.

Straightaway, the seagull was transformed. But not into a magnificent golden eagle. Incredibly, and disastrously, the seagull turned into a double-decker bus. And because double-decker buses can't fly, it dropped out of the sky, and with an eardrum-bursting shatter, crashed straight through the roof of Halfbottle and Son's ice cream factory in Teapot Street.

"Ooops," said Keith. "Not quite what I had in mind, but you get the picture."

Colin was impressed. He didn't know much about boring old seagulls or magnificent golden eagles, but the sight of a double-decker bus dropping out of the sky and flattening an ice cream factory was the most spectacular disaster he had ever seen. Keith was clearly a genie of great magnificence – and he was offering Colin three wishes.

Now, if any normal person were to be offered three wishes, they would probably wish for great wealth, or great beauty or great wisdom. But Colin Crumbly wasn't a normal person. He was too disastrous for that.

No. Colin thought and thought about his three wishes, and all he could think about was his classmates, running away in panic before he had a

chance to open his lunch box. And yet, Colin liked his classmates. And he wanted them to like *him.*

"Can you make my classmates like me?" he asked.

"Course I can, Colin, my little jellied eel," said Keith.

And he jiggled his lemon yellow eyebrow...

When lunch-time was over, Mrs Stick walked back into her classroom, and the weirdest sight met her eyes. A sight so weird she simply couldn't believe it. She polished her spectacles, but the weird sight was still there. She polished her eyeballs, but the weird sight wouldn't go away. Something weird really had happened in her classroom, and she didn't like it one bit.

"WHAT ON EARTH'S GOING ON?" she shrieked in a strange voice that sounded like she had a hundred frogs stuck in her throat.

Nobody replied . . . but Colin Crumbly gulped loudly. *He* knew what was going on.

It was that Lemonade Genie. Keith. He had made Colin's wish come true. He had made all Colin Crumbly's classmates like him. The trouble was, he hadn't just made Colin Crumbly's classmates *like* him. He had made Colin Crumbly's classmates *exactly* like him. That stupid Lemonade Genie had turned everyone in Mrs Stick's class into Colin Crumblies.

There were now thirty-three Colin Crumblies in Mrs Stick's class. And the terrifying thing was, thirty-three Colin Crumblies could be thirty-three times more disastrous than one Colin Crumbly.

"OOOOOOH NOOOOOO!" shrieked Mrs Stick, as all the huge horribleness of what had happened began to sink in.

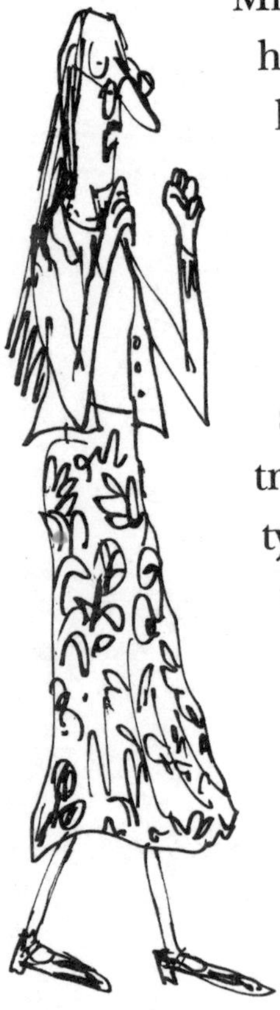

In front of her, there were thirty-three Colin Crumblies, falling off their chairs, knocking over their tables, spilling their paint pots, tripping over each other's feet, tying each other's shoelaces together, tucking their flapping shirt-tails into each other's trousers, sneezing all over each other, and finally, horribly, disastrously, blowing their noses – without handkerchiefs.

And the nose-blows were long and loud, like a great nose-blowing symphony played by a disgusting thirty-three-piece nose-blowing orchestra.

Mrs Stick tried hard not to faint, but it was difficult. Her head felt as if it was filled with bubbles, and her heart and stomach had sunk into her shoes.

"It's my worst nightmare... It's come true..." she gasped. "While I've been having my lunch, there's been an invasion of Colin Crumblies... Colin Crumblies have taken over the world..."

"Sorry, Mrs Stick," said one of the Colin Crumblies, as it trod on her foot and accidentally poked a pencil up her nose.

"Sorry, Mrs Stick," said another of the Colin Crumblies, as it accidentally roller-skated across the floor on a wax crayon, lunged forward and got its tongue stuck in Mrs Stick's ear.

"Sorry, Mrs Stick," said yet another Colin Crumbly, as it accidentally poured pink paint over Geronimo the class gerbil.

"COLIN! DON'T YOU DARE!" shrieked Mrs Stick, as a fourth Colin Crumbly picked up the gerbil, shook it, squeezed it, and wrung all the wet paint out of it.

It was only then that she fainted. Confused, terrified, and splattered all over in pink paint. And as she fainted, the last thing she saw was a classroom full of Colin Crumbly faces, all saying: "Sorry, Mrs Stick."

3
The Enormous Mistake

Afternoon playtime came and the Colin Crumblies stampeded towards the playground like a herd of drunk elephants.

All except the one real Colin Crumbly.

He had looked on in horror at all the disasters his classmates had caused. And now that he was on his own again, all he wanted to do was grab Keith by the throat and shake him until he popped everywhere.

"So, what do you fancy for your second wish, Colin, my old dog and bone?" Keith asked, jingling his lemon ear-rings cheerily.

"My second wish?" snapped Colin.

"My second wish? You really think I dare ask for a second wish after the complete disaster you made of my first wish? I dread to think what you might do."

"Er, yeah, sorry about that. But anyone can make a mistake. I'm only a genie, you know. I may be almighty, but I'm not perfect. Give me another chance. Just say the word. All I have to do is jiggle my eyebrow," said Keith, jiggling his eyebrow.

And in the distance, there was an almighty crash, as a double-decker bus fell out of the sky and into the wig display at Drizzle's Hairdressers in Milkjug Road.

"Now, how did I do that?" wondered Keith, staring out of the window, worriedly.

Colin knew he really oughtn't make another wish in case it turned out as disastrously as the first one. But he simply couldn't help it.

"I just want all my classmates to be normal. That's all. Do you think you can manage that, Keith?"

"No problem, Colin, my little brown jug."

And Keith jiggled a lemon yellow eyebrow...

Screams of terror came from the playground. And there were dreadful crashing sounds. The sounds of a thousand accidents happening, one after another. And there were loud thundering voices. Like the voices of great gods, booming important words down from the heavens to the little people below. And the voices said: "SORRY. SORRY EVERYBODY. VERY SORRY."

Colin ran into the playground, and what he saw there froze the very bones in his body.

Terrified children were running this way and that. Terrified teachers were running this way and that. Terrified Colin Crumblies were running this way and that. And the terrified children and the terrified teachers were running away from the terrified Colin Crumblies, while the terrified Colin Crumblies were running away from each other. And the

reason everyone was running was simple: something terrifying had happened to the thirty-two Colin Crumblies.

Incredibly, disastrously, they had grown... and grown... into thirty-two GIANT Colin Crumblies.

The one real Colin Crumbly stared in disbelief. His mouth fell open and a pathetic sort of whimpering noise dribbled off his tongue.

"Oh, Keith..." he said, at last. "*Normal.* I said *normal.* I wished for my classmates to be *normal.*"

"Oh. *Normal,*" giggled Keith. "I thought you said *enormous.*"

Now, having a whole classroom full of Colin Crumblies was disastrous enough. But having thirty-two GIANT Colin Crumblies, all terrified and crashing about in the school playground... *that* was *really* disastrous.

Walls got tripped over and demolished. Railings got trodden on and flattened. Windows got smashed. And everywhere, all kinds of damage got done, and it all happened accidentally.

One of the giant Colin Crumblies got accidentally tangled up in the telephone wires, tripped and fell, nose-first, SMACK! on top of Mr Bleach, the headmaster.

"Get this revolting nostril off me this instant!" shrieked Mr Bleach, who didn't enjoy finding himself unexpectedly stuck inside someone else's nose.

But nobody took any notice of him. Everyone was too busy running away from all the terrible things that were happening.

It was as if a small earthquake had struck Moonwood County Primary School – and it was all the fault of those thirty-two giant Colin Crumblies.

"SORRY. VERY SORRY EVERYBODY," they said, as they all crashed about, confused and panicking.

Moments later, sirens started sounding, and ambulances and police cars and fire engines appeared around the school, in Teapot Street and Milkjug Road.

Colin hid behind the bicycle shed and watched everything. He was struck dumb with shock. All the words he had ever known had flown away out of his ears. All he could do was stare, shake his head and, every now and again, giggle stupidly.

"THIS IS SUPERINTENDENT BRICKHOUSE SPEAKING," came a voice over a loudspeaker.

The earth shuddered, as the massive Colin Crumblies tried their very best to keep their huge clumping feet still.

One of the Colin Crumblies sneezed a monumental sneeze. It sounded like the thunderous waves of a mighty ocean, and there was a huge gust of wind which blew some policemen halfway down Teapot Street.

Another Colin Crumbly blew his nose – without a handkerchief. It felt like being caught in the blast of a sticky green storm, and everyone around him said, "UUUUUGH!"

Behind the bicycle shed, Colin could bear to watch no more. He closed his eyes tight, and hoped he was dreaming. He tried hard to make himself wake up. But when he opened his eyes again, everything was still as dreadful as it had been just before.

And he had the feeling it was about to get worse.

4

The Crashing Giants

"Cor, those giant Colin Crumblies are a bit disastrous," said a familiar voice close to Colin's ear.

"Keith. . ." groaned Colin. "What are you doing here? I was hoping I'd never see you again."

"Aw, you don't mean that, do you, Colin, my fat old trout? I can't go yet. You've got one wish left, remember."

"One wish left?" snapped Colin. "One wish left? You think I'm going to make another wish after all the trouble my first two wishes caused? Keith, I am absolutely definitely *never* asking you for any more wishes so don't you *dare* do that wiggly thing with your eyebrow ever again."

Keith shrugged.

And as he shrugged, a double-decker bus sailed elegantly over their heads and crash-landed three streets away, slap-bang on top of Trudge's Toffee Emporium.

"Now, how did I do *that*?" wondered Keith, staring all around at the sky, worriedly.

Just then, one of the giant Colin Crumblies accidentally swallowed a whole flock of passing geese. They tickled him all the way down to his tummy, and he wriggled, and twitched, and giggled. Then he coughed, spluttered and spat a whole snowstorm of feathers across the playground.

And then he fell over backwards and squashed Superintendent Brickhouse's police car.

"RIGHT. THAT'S IT. YOU'VE HAD YOUR WARNING," shrieked Superintendent Brickhouse.

And while Superintendent Brickhouse wondered how on earth he could possibly stop these giant Colin Crumblies being totally disastrous, Colin did some wondering of his own.

And the more he wondered, the more he realised there was only one thing to do.

"Keith..." he began. "Now listen to me carefully. I don't want you to get this wrong. I don't want any more mistakes. I just want you to turn all the giant Colin Crumblies back into my classmates. Can you do that for me?"

"Easy-peasy," grinned Keith, raising a lemon yellow eyebrow...

But then, he paused.

"Actually, Colin," he said quietly, "no, I can't do that."

Colin stared at him.

"What do you mean?" he asked.

"Turning people back into themselves is a very complicated operation," said Keith, glumly. And the bright yellow spikes of his hair seemed to droop with sadness. "You need a Grandmaster Certificate in Advanced Genieography to do it. And I've just got my Beginner's Badge."

Colin's heart skipped a hundred beats.

"But... These are my classmates," he stammered. "They don't have to be giant Colin Crumblies for ever...do they?"

"Course not!" laughed Keith. "I could always turn them into magnificent golden eagles. Or double-decker buses."

"But... You turned my classmates into these giant Colin Crumblies," Colin stammered. "All these disasters wouldn't have happened if it weren't for you. This is all *your* fault. So you can just turn everyone back into themselves RIGHT NOW."

"Well, I'm sorry, Colin, my little treacle tart, but all this is *your* fault, not mine," Keith said crossly. "I turned your classmates into thirty-two giant versions of *you*. And if you weren't such a disastrous person, all these giant disasters would never have happened. Now you think about *that*, Colin Crumbly."

Colin thought.

And he realised it was true. It *was* all his fault. All these terrible things had happened because of him, Colin Crumbly, the Undisputed Disaster Champion of the World.

If Keith had turned his classmates into thirty-two giant versions of Colin's mum, they wouldn't have been disastrous at all. They would have just sat quietly in a corner somewhere, doing jigsaws. But then again, thirty-two giant versions of Colin's dad, the man with the pongiest feet on the planet, would have been an even bigger disaster. Everyone in Moonwood would have been ponged to death.

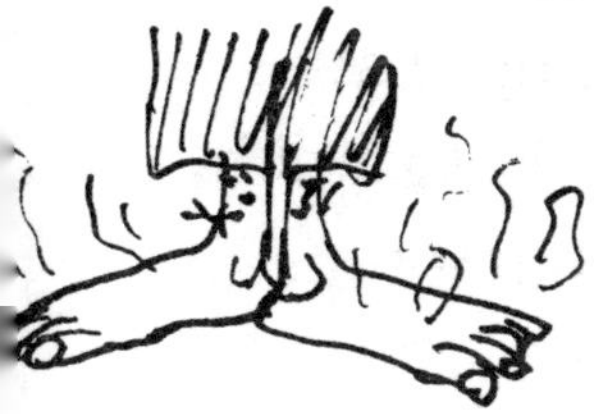

At that moment, one of the giant Colin Crumblies accidentally got a small boy stuck up his trouser leg. He stood on one foot and tried to shake him out. But because he wasn't very good at standing on one foot, the giant fell over and flattened the bicycle sheds right in front of Colin and the genie.

"I'm . . . sorry I'm so disastrous," Colin said quietly. "But it's the way I am. I can't help it. I can't even do a simple thing like make three wishes without destroying my entire school. All I wanted was for my classmates to like me."

Colin sobbed. And sniffed. And blew his nose. Without a handkerchief.

And Keith suddenly felt sorry for the boy. He took a deep breath...but he didn't speak. Instead, he jiggled his lemon yellow eyebrow.

He jiggled it harder than he had ever jiggled it before.

Nothing happened.

He tried jiggling both eyebrows, up and down, side to side, round in circles.

Still nothing happened.

He tried jiggling his whole face.

He shook it.

He twisted it.

He squashed it.

He squirmed it.

He stretched it.

He pulled a hundred of the ugliest faces ever seen.

And suddenly...

There was a hissing noise. Tiny sparks began to crackle all over him. Silver flames leapt from the ends of his lemon yellow spiky hair. There was a rumble of thunder. The earth shook.

Across the playground, the giant Colin Crumblies shouted "OOOO-EEER!" and began to rock, wobble, and topple…

"LOOK OUT!" shrieked Superintendent Brickhouse.

And everyone ran, screaming, terrified of being squished beneath a Colin Crumbly.

All except one small girl. She didn't seem to be able to move. Colin watched in horror as a massive Colin Crumbly tumbled towards her.

A dangerous thought entered Colin's head. He could save that girl. If only he wasn't so disastrous...

The next moment, he was running, straighter, swifter and surer than he had ever run before. For the first time in his life, Colin's arms and legs seemed to be doing exactly what he wanted them to do. His heart bursting with excitement, he ran hard and fast…

and snatched up the terrified girl.

"I've got you!" he cried triumphantly.

Then he fell over.

But because he was Colin Crumbly, he didn't just fall over. He stumbled and sprawled like a giraffe on roller-skates. His legs did a crazy tangled-up tap-dance. And with the bewildered girl tucked under his arm, he staggered and skidded and crashed in a heap behind a row of dustbins.

There was a monstrous clap of thunder, like the sound of the whole world cracking in two. Or maybe it was just the sound of a row of dustbins clattering.

And then, there was silence.

"You saved me," said the girl at last. "You saved my life! I've been saved... by COLIN CRUMBLY!"

Colin got to his feet slowly. He was covered in bumps and bruises and felt sore all over. But when he looked up, he saw... the giant Colin Crumblies had gone.

His classmates were themselves again. And they were all staring at him. In fact, everyone seemed to be staring at him. At first, in disbelief. But then they smiled, and clapped, and cheered.

5
The Golden Shock

They seemed a little dizzy and confused, but otherwise, Colin's classmates looked exactly how they were supposed to look. You would certainly never have guessed that, moments before, they had all been giant Colin Crumblies. (Except, perhaps, for the one who had the small boy stuck up his trouser leg. Now that he was back down to normal size again, it simply looked as if two small boys were stuck inside one pair of trousers.)

Everything else about Moonwood County Primary School was in a bit of a mess. The playground was scattered with twisted metal, splintered wood, broken bricks, bruised policemen, and bamboozled teachers.

Superintendent Brickhouse picked himself up from the bottom of a pile of policemen, and stared around him, completely baffled by the disappearance of the giant Colin Crumblies.

Mr Bleach the headmaster simply looked dazed, as you would expect of a man who had just spent the last few minutes jammed up a giant's nose.

But the children of Moonwood County Primary School were happy. For most of them, having a disaster area for a playground was a dream come true.

And Colin Crumbly was the happiest of all.

"I saved that girl," he said to himself. "I was brave... I was fearless... I was still disastrous, but I was a hero! Did you see me, Keith? KEITH?"

Keith was lying flat on his back, exhausted, his face covered in soot, his huge yellow hair smoking like a fire that had just gone out.

"Sorry, Colin, mate... I'm afraid I was too busy blowing myself up," he croaked.

And a cloud of yellow smoke puffed out of his mouth.

"But you were tremendous!" said Colin. "You said you couldn't do it, but you did! You turned everyone back into themselves!"

"My head feels like it's gone off like a fireworks display," Keith groaned. "I don't think I *ever* want a Grandmaster Certificate in Advanced Genieography. I'm all wished out."

"Fancy a game of *Space Masters,* Colin?" one of Colin's classmates asked suddenly. "I'll be Captain Doom, and you can be Disasterboy."

Colin froze, as if he had had the greatest shock of his life.

Had he heard correctly? Had one of his classmates really asked His Imperial Disastrousness, Colin Crumbly, to play?

"Come on, Colin! It'll be fun!"

Colin didn't know what to say. His mouth opened, but his voice wouldn't work. Instead, he sneezed, long and hard all over his shoes.

"You know, I think I could be very good at being Disasterboy," smiled Colin.

And he and his classmates laughed.

And while they were busy laughing and becoming friends, the air filled with explosions, as if somewhere in space almighty corks were popping.

Colin looked up and saw a strange Lemonade Genie-shaped cloud, made up of billions of silver bubbles. And as he watched, the bubbles trailed away and wrote a message across the sky:

Back in the classroom after playtime, Mrs Stick was beginning to feel better. She looked around at the faces of her class, and decided that all those terrifying Colin Crumbly faces she thought she had seen earlier must have been part of some horrible dream. There was certainly only one Colin Crumbly in front of her now – and even he didn't look quite like his usual self. By this time of the day, he normally had about twenty-seven plasters all over him, at least one black eye and a school gate stuck over his head. But today, he looked strangely... different. He was battered and bruised as always, but he was... smiling.

"Colin... are you all right?" she asked, worriedly.

"I've never felt better in my life, Mrs Stick," replied Colin, happily.

"But, Mrs Stick... *We* don't feel very well at all..." said his classmates weakly.

They all stood up and turned round, and bent over.

Mrs Stick gasped at

the extraordinary sight before her.

Out of the bottom of everyone in the class – everyone except Colin Crumbly, that was – a tail was growing. There were thirty-two of them. Splendid feathery tails, all glistening with sprinkles of gold. The tails of magnificent golden eagles.

Mrs Stick stared and stared. Then, softly and silently, she fainted.

"Oh no..." groaned Colin. "KEITH!"